Fun China

CHINESE FOOD

Written by **Alice Ma**
Illustrated by **Sheung Wong**
Reviewed by **Judith Malmsbury**

Sun Ya Publications (HK) Ltd.
www.sunya.com.hk

After a long day at school, Charlie and Ying Ying
went home hoping to find some food in the kitchen.
As they open the fridge,
a wise and gentle creature appears.
It is Dragon C from China!

Peking Duck is a yummy and famous Chinese dish.
It is loved by people all over the world.
Would you like to try it? Let's make it together.

First, take a thin pancake.
Then, put a slice of the duck on it.
Next, add some shredded vegetables
and a savoury sauce, and wrap it up.
Now you can enjoy its amazing taste in your mouth!
Want more? Don't miss out on the duck soup!
It is rich in flavor and good for health.

I hope we have Peking duck for Thanksgiving.

Noodles are very popular in China.
They come in many shapes, from thin and round
to thick and flat. You can eat them in soup
or stir-fried with veggies and meat.

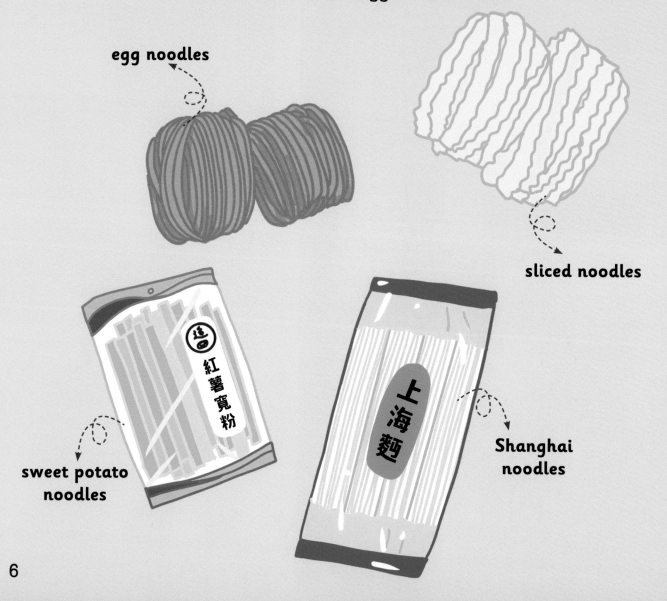

egg noodles

sliced noodles

sweet potato
noodles

紅薯寬粉

上海麵

Shanghai
noodles

In Chinese culture, noodles represent a long life.
The longer, the better!

wonton noodles

fried noodles

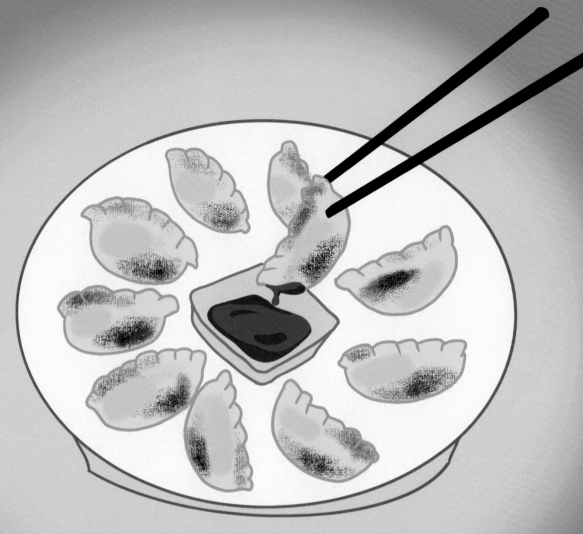

Dumplings are a common food in China
and other Asian countries. They are small pockets
filled with tasty things like meat and vegetables.
Dip them in a sour or savoury sauce.
They will be even yummier.

Dumplings mean being together in Chinese culture.
People share dumplings with family
during important festivals. Boiled, steamed or fried,
dumplings will always make you happy.

Have you heard of dim sum?
It is a style of Chinese food with many small dishes.
We can have steamed buns, spring rolls,
shrimp dumplings and more.
It will be a fun party for our taste buds!

shrimp dumplings

pork dumplings

rice noodle rolls

sesame deep-fried sticky rice balls

different kinds of buns

And the best part? The dishes are small.
So, we can try many of them without feeling too full!

We can buy them from street vendors at festivals.
The vendors put sweet and sour red berries on a stick,
and cover them with sugar syrup.
They are fun to eat and taste delicious.
Everyone loves them in China!

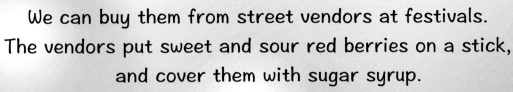

There are also sugar-coated kiwis,
strawberries and pineapples.
They look like
a beautiful rainbow!

Let's take a break and drink some Chinese tea.
Chinese tea is enjoyed all over the world.

I like to have tea with some honey.

14

Try some of the most popular Chinese teas,
like green tea, black tea and jasmine tea.
They each have a unique taste and are good for your health.
Take a sip and enjoy the wonderful world of Chinese tea!

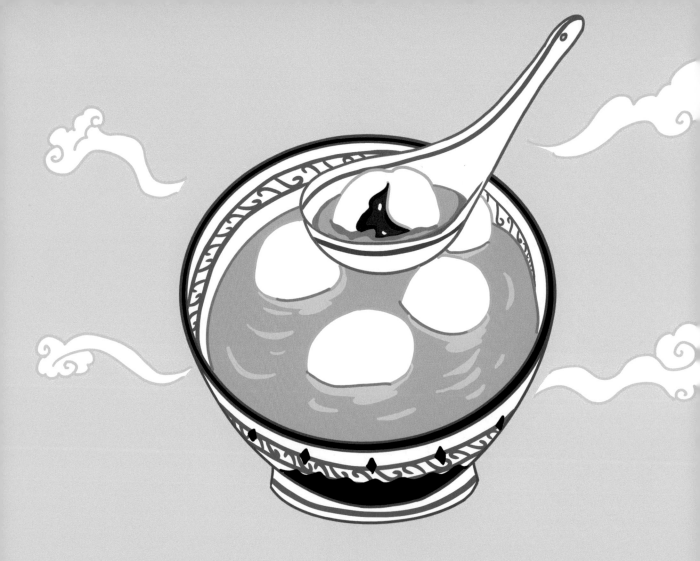

If you want something sweet, try sticky rice balls.
They are a yummy Chinese dessert
with sweet fillings such as red bean paste.
When boiled, they are perfect in a warm soup.

Sticky rice balls mean being together, just like dumplings.
They are a great food to share with family
during special times.
Try them at your next family gathering!

Look up at the night sky — it is a full moon.
It looks like a Chinese festive pastry called mooncakes!
These yummy cakes are filled with a special sweet paste
and salted egg yolk.

Families usually eat mooncakes and look at the moon in mid-autumn. Now, there are many different types of mooncakes to try. For example, we can have ice cream mooncakes and mixed nuts mooncakes. Which one do you want to try the most?

I would like to have a chocolate chip mooncake.

Let's try another Chinese festive food —
sticky rice dumplings. These treats are wrapped in leaves
and shaped like pyramids.

They are made with sticky rice, pork, mushrooms
and other yummy food. When you eat them,
you will be surprised by how delicious they taste.

Get ready for hot pot!
It is a special Chinese dish
full of fun. You can cook your
own meats, vegetables and
noodles in a boiling broth.

deep-fried bean curd rolls

all kinds of fish and meat balls

Hot pot is not just a meal.
It is an enjoyable dining experience
with family and friends.
Come enjoy the food
that warms your heart inside and out.

Charlie and Ying Ying enjoyed every bite of the Chinese food. They went back home with Dragon C.

As they say goodbye, Charlie and Ying Ying know
that they have learned to love Chinese food.
Also, they are happy to make a new friend with Dragon C.

English - Chinese Glossary of Chinese Food

Peking duck
TC 北京烤鴨
SC 北京烤鸭
🔊 Běijīng kǎo yā

Noodles
TC 麵條
SC 面条
🔊 miàn tiáo

Dumplings
TC 餃子
SC 饺子
🔊 jiǎo zi

Dim sum
TC 點心
SC 点心
🔊 diǎn xin

Sugar-coated haws
TC 冰糖葫蘆
SC 冰糖葫芦
🔊 bīng táng hú lu

Chinese tea

TC 中國茶

SC 中国茶

 Zhōngguó chá

Mooncakes

TC 月餅

SC 月饼

 yuè bing

Sticky rice dumpling

TC 糭子

SC 糭子

 zòng zi

Sticky rice balls

TC 湯圓

SC 汤圆

 tāng yuán

Hot pot

TC 火鍋

SC 火锅

 huǒ guō

Fun China
Chinese Food

Author
Alice Ma

Illustrator
Sheung Wong

Reviewer
Judith Malmsbury

Executive Editor
Tracy Wong

Graphic Designer
Aspen Kwok

Publisher
Sun Ya Publications (HK) Ltd.
18/F, North Point Industrial Building, 499 King's Road, Hong Kong
Tel: (852) 2138 7998   Fax: (852) 2597 4003
Website: https://www.sunya.com.hk
E-mail: marketing@sunya.com.hk

Distributor
SUP Publishing Logistics (HK) Ltd.
16/F, Tsuen Wan Industrial Centre, 220-248 Texaco Road,
Tsuen Wan, N.T., Hong Kong
Tel: (852) 2150 2100   Fax: (852) 2407 3062
E-mail: info@suplogistics.com.hk

Printer
C & C Offset Printing Co., Ltd.
36 Ting Lai Road, Tai Po, N.T., Hong Kong

Edition
First published in October 2023
Third impression printed in July 2024

ISBN: 978-962-08-8259-3
© 2023 Sun Ya Publications (HK) Ltd.
18/F, North Point Industrial Building, 499 King's Road, Hong Kong
Published in Hong Kong SAR, China
Printed in China